860

What's your bravest moment?

✪

"I got a shot at the doctor's office. Then they gave me a sticker." —Noa

"Going to school all by myself, without my big sister there." —Brooke

"[Going] to sleepaway camp, which meant being away from my parents for seven whole weeks!" —Harrison

"My first big dance performance." —Gus

"It's going to be riding on a hoverboard." —Charlie

Visit all the states with
Finn and Molly in

MAGIC ON THE MAP 4

ESCAPE FROM CAMP CALIFORNIA

COURTNEY SHEINMEL
& BIANCA TURETSKY

illustrated by STEVIE LEWIS

A STEPPING STONE BOOK™

Random House 🏠 New York

For Lucy Ann and Oliver David
—C.S.

For Charlie and Freya
—B.T.

Text copyright © 2020 by Courtney Sheinmel and Bianca Turetsky
Cover art and interior illustrations copyright © 2020 by Stevie Lewis

Visit us on the Web!
rhcbooks.com

Educators and librarians, for a variety of teaching tools,
visit us at RHTeachersLibrarians.com

Library of Congress Cataloging-in-Publication Data
Names: Sheinmel, Courtney, author. | Turetsky, Bianca, author. |
Lewis, Stevie, illustrator.
Title: Escape from Camp California / Courtney Sheinmel and Bianca Turetsky;
illustrated by Stevie Lewis.
Description: New York: Random House, [2020] | Series: Magic on the map; #4
"A Stepping Stone Book." | Audience: Ages 6–9.
Summary: The magical RV takes twins Finn and Molly to Northern California,
where they help keep campers safe during a wildfire.
Identifiers: LCCN 2019038358 | ISBN 978-1-9848-9572-1 (trade)
ISBN 978-1-9848-9573-8 (lib. bdg.) | ISBN 978-1-9848-9574-5 (ebook)
Subjects: CYAC: Recreational vehicles—Fiction. | Magic—Fiction. |
Brothers and sisters—Fiction. | Twins—Fiction. | Camps—Fiction. |
Wildfires—Fiction. | Fires—Fiction. | California, Northern—Fiction.
Classification: LCC PZ7.S54124 Es 2020 | DDC [Fic]—dc23

Printed in the United States of America
10 9 8 7 6 5 4 3 2 1

This book has been officially leveled by using the F&P Text Level Gradient™
Leveling System.

Random House Children's Books supports the First Amendment
and celebrates the right to read.

Contents

PROLOGUE

On the last day of second grade, twins Finn and Molly Parker came home to find a camper in their driveway. It was white with orange and yellow stripes, a rounded roof, and three windows on each side. It looked just like an ordinary camper.

That night, Molly and Finn couldn't sleep. They snuck outside to check out the camper. Finn climbed into the driver's seat and spun the wheel around. He and Molly knew that they couldn't go anywhere. They didn't have the keys. And besides, they were too young to drive!

But something weird happened . . . the camper started *talking* to them. It wasn't an ordinary camper, after all—it had a PET!

Not a pet like a cat or a dog, or even an iguana. *This* PET stood for:

Planet

Earth

Transporter.

PET explained that it used the *information superhighway* to travel anywhere in the world, in a matter of seconds. And then, faster than you could say, "Buckle up," the camper took off!

When it landed, the doors popped open.

"I'll be back when your work here is done," PET said, and it shut down.

Molly and Finn didn't know where they were or what in the world their work was. But they knew there was only one way to find out, and they headed outside.

Where will the magic camper take Finn and Molly next? You'll just have to keep reading to find out. . . .

Chapter 1

BLUE AND GOLD

Molly Parker was finishing up her latest friendship bracelet when her twin brother, Finn, knocked on her door.

"Come in," Molly said. She spoke softly so her parents wouldn't overhear. It was very important that they think Molly and Finn were both sound asleep.

Finn opened the door. "Ready to go?" he whispered.

"Almost," Molly said. "Just one more knot."

Finn tiptoed into the room and stood over his sister. "Blue and gold," he said. "Cool. Did you pick that for the Kansas City Royals?"

"Huh?" Molly said.

"Or the Milwaukee Brewers?" he asked.

Molly snipped the end of the bracelet with her scissors. "I don't know what you're talking about," she said.

"Baseball teams, obviously," Finn said. "The Royals' and the Brewers' colors are both blue and gold."

"Oh," Molly said. "No, I wasn't thinking about the teams. I just like the way the colors look together." She held the bracelet to her wrist. "Tie this on for me?"

"We have to go," Finn said.

"Tie this for me, and then we'll go," she said.

"Fine," Finn said.

"Don't knot it too tightly," Molly warned. "I need to be able to take it off so I can give it away."

"I know, I know," Finn said with a roll of his eyes.

"But don't tie it too loosely, either," Molly added. "I don't want it to fall off."

"There," Finn said. "I tied it just right. *Now* can we go?"

"Yep!" Molly said, a little too loudly.

"Shh," Finn warned.

Molly pretended to zip her mouth shut. She put on her bunny slippers. Then she and Finn tiptoed out to the hallway. Their

parents' door was shut. The coast was clear. They walked downstairs, as quiet as mice.

"What would Mom and Dad think if we told them that we'd been to three states since the beginning of summer vacation?" Finn whispered.

"They'd never believe us," Molly whispered back.

She pushed open the front door. Finn gently closed it behind them. They ran across the lawn, yanked open the camper door, and scrambled in.

"We made it," Finn said. "Phew!"

Molly walked to the back of the camper, where a map of the world was pinned onto a bulletin board. She and Finn had put four pushpins in the map so far—one in their home state of Ohio, where they'd lived their whole lives. The three other pins were in each of the places they'd gone: Colorado, New York, and Texas.

Molly touched the tip of her finger to the pushpins and felt little sparks.

"Come on," Finn called from the front, where he was already sitting in the passenger seat. "It's your turn. We can't get started till you're up here! You know how strict PET is about these rules!"

Molly jogged toward the front. "Do you think they're PET's rules or Professor Vega's rules?" she asked.

Professor Vega worked at the college with Finn and Molly's dad. She had owned the camper before trading it for Mr. Parker's car. But Finn and Molly didn't know anything else about her.

Finn shrugged. Molly sat down in the driver's seat. As soon as she did, the TV screen lit up—first a flash of white, then blue, then red letters that spelled out "HELLO AGAIN."

"Hi, PET!" Finn cried.

"Hello, Finn," a robotic voice replied.

"Hello from me, too," Molly said.

"Molly, I'm glad to hear your voice," PET

said. "Have you thought about where you'd like to go?"

"Yes, I have," Molly said. "I want to go where help is needed."

"Wherever we go, help will be needed," Finn said. "PET told us that last time."

"That's right," PET said. "Lots of destinations to choose from, but you can only pick one of them. And time's a-wasting."

The word "TICKTOCK" flashed on PET's screen.

"I can't decide," Molly said. "Will you pick for me?"

"You bet I—" Finn started.

"Not you," Molly said. "*PET.* You and I don't know who needs help the most."

"Hmm . . . ," PET said. "Where to go? Where to go? We could go north . . . or we could go east . . . but, yes, I believe I have just the place. . . ."

"I bet it's Kansas City!" Finn cried.

"Do you mean the Kansas City in Kansas or Missouri?" Molly asked.

"I don't know," Finn said. "Maybe neither. We could be going to the state of Milwaukee."

"Milwaukee isn't a state," Molly said.

"Sure it is," Finn said.

"No, it's a city in the state of Wisconsin."

"Close enough," Finn said.

"Buckle up, buckaroos!" PET called, and they were off.

Chapter 2

EUREKA

"Check out the feathers on those birds!" Finn said.

Molly leaned over to look out her brother's window. The birds outside had dark feathers sticking straight up from their heads.

"Ooh," she said. "They must be a type of quail. It's weird that they're flying."

"They're birds," Finn said. "They have wings. Of course they're flying."

"Just because a bird has wings doesn't mean it likes to fly," Molly said. "It just so happens that quail would rather run along the ground. Unless something on the ground scares them. Then they can fly up super fast."

Finn glanced down. "Everything looks fine on the ground," he said. "Check out those flowers." He pointed to the rolling hills, which were dotted with thousands—maybe millions—of tiny orange flowers.

"And check that out," Molly said. She pointed toward a body of water.

"Oh, is that the ocean again?" Finn asked. "Like when we went to New York?"

"Nah," Molly said. "That's not big enough to be an ocean."

"It looks pretty big to me," Finn said.

"But there's a bridge," Molly said. "Oceans

don't usually have bridges, and this one . . . oh my goodness!"

"What?"

"The bridge is orange, same as the flowers," Molly said. "You know what that means?"

Finn gave his sister a blank stare. "Uh . . ."

"It means that bridge is the GOLDEN GATE BRIDGE!" she cried.

"Cool," Finn said.

"Cool?" Molly cried. "That's all you have to say about being in California?"

"California?" Finn said. "Holy guacamole!"

"That's more like it," Molly said.

But now the Golden Gate Bridge was behind them. The camper flew over a forest dense with trees that stretched over a hundred feet in the air. They dropped down into a small clearing and landed with a thud.

"I'll be back—" PET started.

"We know, we know," Finn said. "You'll be back when our work here is done."

PET's screen went dark and the camper doors popped open.

"Ready to go?" Molly asked.

"You bet I am," Finn said.

The twins stepped onto the mossy floor of the forest. Molly noticed that Finn's pajamas had been replaced with navy shorts and a white T-shirt. "EUREKA" was written across the front of his shirt in gold letters. When Molly glanced down, she saw that she was in the exact same outfit.

"We're dressed like twins," she said.

"We *are* twins," Finn said.

"Yeah, but we're not twins who dress the same," Molly said. "This must be some kind of uniform. What is the Eureka team?"

"Don't know," Finn said. Suddenly, he felt nervous. He reached up and checked his head. *Phew.* His trusty Moonwalkers baseball cap was still there, right where it belonged.

"You don't know something about *baseball*?" Molly asked, incredulous.

"I know all the major-league teams," Finn said. "But there are way more minor-league and Little League teams. Even the biggest baseball expert in the world wouldn't be able to memorize all of them. Besides, these could be uniforms for a completely different sport. One where you'd need to be wearing these." He lifted up a foot to show off his hiking boots.

"Maybe we're supposed to hike that mountain over there," Molly said. "That could be where our work is."

"But then why did PET drop us off here, in the forest?" Finn asked.

Molly shrugged.

"Hello?" a voice called. "Hello, anyone over there?"

Seconds later, a woman wearing the same EUREKA T-shirt and navy shorts walked through a break in the trees.

"Hey, friends," she said. "What are you doing over here?"

"Uh . . . ," Finn said.

He glanced back toward the camper, but it had disappeared.

"Do you need any help?" the woman asked.

"Actually, we were just going to ask you the same thing," Molly said.

"Well, aren't you two kind," the woman

said. "What are your names? I didn't catch them at orientation."

Molly didn't know what orientation the woman was talking about, but she answered the question anyway.

"I'm Molly, and this is my brother, Finn," she said. "We're twins."

"A pleasure to meet you, Molly and Finn. My name is Danielle. Come join me at the lake. Your Camp Eureka friends are finishing up the morning swim."

"Camp?" Molly said. "We're at camp? In California?"

"Well, of course you are," Danielle said, giving Molly a funny look. "You didn't just get dropped here out of nowhere."

The twins shared a glance.

"Ready to go?" Danielle asked. She turned around, and the twins got a glimpse of the back of her T-shirt. There were big gold letters that spelled out "COUNSELOR."

They followed Danielle through the trees into a large clearing.

"Oh wow," Molly said.

Chapter 3

DR. MOLLY PARKER

Danielle and the twins stood beside a gray clapboard boathouse. An enormous blue lake stretched out in front of them. Dozens of campers were swimming, canoeing, kayaking, and stand-up paddleboarding. A couple were even trying to windsurf, though there wasn't very much wind for it.

"Holy guacamole," Finn said.

"You can say that again," Molly told him.

"Holy guacamole," he repeated.

Danielle grinned. "I'd say you two should suit up and get out there, but we don't have a lot of time left for group swim."

"That's okay, but—" Molly said.

"Hey, Danielle," a boy called.

"I'm being paged," Danielle told the twins. "Hold that thought. I'll be back in a jiff."

Finn turned around in a circle, taking everything in. Then he looked at his sister. "What should we do while we wait?" he asked. "There's a rock wall over there, an art studio over there, and tennis courts over there. I can't see what's all the way over there—maybe it's a baseball diamond!"

"I think we should stay here and watch the swimmers," Molly said. "Our work could be rescuing someone who goes out too deep."

"I doubt it," Finn said. "See those life-guards? They're watching the swimmers."

"We should watch them anyway, in case the sun gets in the lifeguards' eyes. They'll need us to shout and alert them."

"Well then, let's sit on those rocks," Finn said, pointing to a jetty across the way. He and Molly scrambled over. It wasn't until they got there that they noticed a girl with thick, dark hair sitting in the shadows of a tall tree. Even though she was wearing a bathing suit, both her suit and her hair were dry.

"Is it okay if we join you?" Finn asked.

The girl shrugged. "Sure, I guess," she said.

"Thanks," Finn said. "My name is Finn, by the way."

"And my name's Molly," Molly added.

"I'm Tess," the girl said.

"Hi, Tess," Molly said. She sat down beside her. "Did you just get here, too?"

"What?" Tess said.

"We just got here, so we're too late for group swim," Molly explained.

"Oh," Tess said. "I've been here the whole time. I have a stomachache, so I'm not swimming."

"That stinks," Finn said.

Molly leaned forward. "A stomachache?" she said. "Really?"

Maybe the work they had to do was figure out what was wrong with Tess's stomach!

"Tell me about your stomachache," Molly said.

"Um . . . ," Tess said. "Well, it hurts."

"Hmm. Interesting," Molly said.

Finn rolled his eyes. "*Of course* her stomach hurts, Molly," he said. "She just said she has a stomachache."

"I know, I know," Molly said. "But if it's a certain kind of ache, then it could be her appendix. That's an organ in your body. Sometimes when it hurts, you need to take it out."

"You can't take out one of her organs," Finn said.

"Obviously *I* can't," Molly said. "A doctor would do it. I read a book all about it." She turned back to Tess. "Is your stomachache on the side? Or all over?"

"Um . . . all over?" Tess said. It sounded like a question.

"All over," Molly said. "Hmm. Then it's probably not your appendix. That's on the right side. Maybe it's the gallbladder. . . ."

"Huh?" Finn said, looking confused. But Molly was too lost in thought to explain that the gallbladder was another organ.

TOOT! TOOT!

The lifeguards' whistles broke Molly's concentration. The campers in the water began to swim and paddle toward the shore.

Tess jumped up.

"Wait!" Molly said. "We still need to figure

out what's causing your stomachache."

"It's okay," Tess said. "I'm actually feeling much better. But thanks for your concern." She waved goodbye and headed over to the flagpole, where a crowd was gathering.

"Wow," Molly said. "That was a miraculous recovery."

"Good job, Dr. Parker," Finn said.

CALIFORNIA REPUBLIC

Chapter 4
BUDDIES

Finn and Molly stayed on the jetty till the very last camper was safely out of the water. Then they ran across the sand and joined Danielle and the other campers by the flagpole. A white flag was hanging down from the top. When the breeze briefly kicked it up, the twins caught a glimpse of a large brown bear in the center.

"Hey, friends!" Danielle called out. "We're

going on a nature hike up Lake Point Trail!"

"Awesome," Finn said. "I wanted to put these hiking boots to good use."

"I promise that you and your hiking boots will get a good workout," Danielle said. "But before we head out, there are a few rules. Make sure to always stay with the group. Don't wander off the trail. It is easy to get lost in the redwood trees."

"We don't have redwoods back home in Harvey Falls, Ohio," Molly whispered to her brother.

"I know that," Finn whispered back.

"Everyone will pick a buddy," Danielle went on. "You should know where your buddy is at all times."

"Will you be my buddy?" Molly asked her brother.

"Hmm . . . let me think about that for a minute . . . ," Finn said.

"Finn!" Molly cried.

"Just kidding! Of course I will," Finn said.

"Raise your hand if you don't have a buddy yet, so we can pair you up with someone," Danielle said.

Tess was the only one to raise her hand.

"Ah," Danielle said. "We must have an odd number of campers, so . . ."

"Tess can come with my brother and me, if she wants," Molly called out. "That is, if that's all right to have a group of three."

"It sure is," Danielle said. "Nice work, Molly and Finn."

The twins smiled at each other. Maybe their work was easy this time. Maybe Tess needed a friend and that's why they were there.

Danielle led the group to the beginning of the trail. Molly, Finn, and Tess stayed toward the back. The twins wanted to keep an eye out for any stragglers—just in case.

"Thanks for letting me join your pair," Tess said. "I was afraid I was going to have to be Danielle's buddy. She's super nice, but . . ."

"But it's better to buddy up with campers, not counselors," Finn finished.

"Exactly," Tess said. "The truth is, I don't have many friends here. I was up in the tree-house when they did the welcome game in the lake on the first day."

"Oh wow, there's a treehouse?" Finn asked.

"Yep. It's by the ropes course," Tess said. "You can see the whole camp from up there. I'll show you later, if you want."

"That'd be great," Molly said.

"Hey, friends, did you hear that?" Danielle called from the front of the group.

Molly, Finn, and Tess stopped talking. The other campers stopped talking, too. But no one heard anything. Just the usual birds chirping and the faint sound of wind in the trees.

"What is it?" a boy finally asked.

"The glorious sound of nature," Danielle answered. "Hear it. See it. Smell it. Feel it."

Molly closed her eyes and let the sun hit her cheeks. She took a big gulp of fresh air. Then Finn pulled on her arm. She opened her eyes again and followed the crowd deeper into the woods. Towering trees shaded the path, but speckles of light came in through the canopy of leaves. Danielle shared facts about redwood trees. Like how they could grow over three hundred feet tall and live up to two thousand years—among the biggest and the oldest trees on earth!

"Hey, friends, look over here," Danielle called. She knelt down next to a patch of yellow and brown grass.

"It looks dead," a girl with a thick, dark braid said.

"Exactly, Serafina," Danielle replied. She

stood up and brushed the grass from her knees. "Because of climate change, we've had less rainfall. We all have to start taking better care of our environment if we want our plants to keep growing."

The campers continued up the twisty path. Orange-gold wildflowers, like the ones the twins had seen out of PET's windshield, grew along the edges.

"What's cool about being here in the forest is there are no buildings and no cars, so it's almost like we went back in time," Finn said. "Maybe a Brachiosaurus will pop up from behind that tree."

"You know we didn't really go back in time, though," Molly said. "That's not . . ." She stopped herself before she finished her sentence. She was going to say, *That's not what*

PET can do. But she didn't want to talk about PET in front of Tess.

"It's so beautiful," Tess said. "I wish I'd brought my camera."

"Nope," Finn said. "Cameras are too modern for these Jurassic times."

"You're right," Tess said. "I'll have to carve it into the wall when we get back to our cave-bunks."

Finn grinned and took off his Moonwalkers cap. He leaned against an enormous tree trunk to wipe his brow.

"Hey, Finn, look behind you," Molly said.

Finn turned around. His eyes went wide as he read the wooden sign with red painted letters:

"Bears?" Finn cried. "Like the one on the flag?"

"Oh, no," Danielle said. "Our state flag has a California grizzly on it, and those bears are long extinct."

"Phew," Finn said. "I mean, I'm really sorry they're extinct. But I'm glad we're not going to run into them!"

"But black bears are still alive and well," Danielle said. "They tend to stay away from people. We probably won't encounter any. But if we do see one, do not make eye contact with it. Remain calm. Move slowly, and sing."

"Did you just say *sing?*" a tall boy with a mop of red hair asked.

"I sure did, Toby," Danielle said. "It's important to remind bears that you're human. Bears find humans very intimidating."

"You sure they won't think we're their next meal?" Tess asked. "A group of human campers probably looks pretty appetizing to a hungry black bear."

Finn nudged his sister. "Could this be our work—saving the group from a *bear*?"

"I hope not," Molly said. "Hey, Danielle, should we sing now, before we see any bears? That way they won't approach us at all."

"That's a great idea," Tess said.

"It certainly couldn't hurt," Danielle said. "How about the Camp Eureka song?"

The campers—except Molly and Finn—joined in as she began to sing, "Camp Eureka is the best place to make new friends. Wherever we go, whatever we do, we'll be together till the end!"

"How much longer do we have to go?"

Serafina asked. "All this hiking is making me hungry."

"Two more turns, and we'll loop back to the mess hall in time for lunch," Danielle said.

"Just so you know, after lunch we have a group game," Tess told the twins. "And then it's campers' choice. I was thinking about doing tie-dyeing. Wanna come with me?"

"Totally," Molly said. "What do you say, Finn?"

"Oh yeah," he said. "I'll tie-dye a shirt in the Moonwalkers' colors. Do they have gray and blue?"

"They sure do," Tess said.

"Or maybe I'll do orange and black for the San Francisco Giants," he said.

"Let me guess—another baseball team?" Molly asked.

"Yep," Finn said. "Do they have those colors, too?"

"They have every color you can imagine," Tess told him.

"Cool," he said.

What a great assignment from PET—the work of being someone's friend at a summer camp. It didn't feel like work at all.

The path opened up into the sunny green lawn.

"That's the mess hall over there," Tess said. "Race you two!"

She sprinted across the field, with Molly and Finn close at her heels.

Chapter 5

THE MESS HALL

The mess hall smelled like Tater Tots and chicken fingers, kind of like the twins' lunchroom at Harvey Falls Elementary. But way louder. Campers pounded on the wooden tabletops with their fists.

BANG! BANG! BANG!

Molly and Finn would never be allowed to do that at school!

A counselor stood on a chair and shouted

into a bullhorn, calling each table up to get their food.

"Isn't this amazing?" Finn asked.

Molly had her hands over her ears. She couldn't hear him, so she didn't answer.

"That's my usual table over there," Tess said. "You'll sit with me, right?"

"Definitely," Finn said. "Right, Molly? Molly?" He pulled at one of his sister's hands to uncover her right ear. "Is it okay with you if we sit at Tess's table?"

"Uh-huh," Molly said.

As Molly, Finn, and Tess made their way across the room, a table of campers cried out, "Hey, Danielle, let me see you get down!"

Across the room, Danielle jumped up from her seat. She twirled around and shook her hips for all to see.

"D-O-W-N," the room chanted. "That's the way we get down!"

"This is it," Tess said, plopping onto a chair at a long wooden table. "Guys, these are my new friends, Finn and Molly."

"Hi, Finn and Molly!" the kids chorused.

"Hi," the twins said back.

There were two empty chairs at the table—one next to Tess and one across from her. "Which do you want?" Finn asked Molly.

"Wait a second," Molly said. "What was that . . . that thing Danielle just did?"

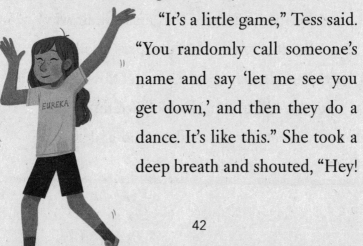

"It's a little game," Tess said. "You randomly call someone's name and say 'let me see you get down,' and then they do a dance. It's like this." She took a deep breath and shouted, "Hey!

Ollie! Let me see you get down!"

A boy at the other end of their table jumped up and did the floss.

"D-O-W-N!" all the other campers cheered. Most of the counselors joined in, too. "That's the way we get down!"

Finn gave Ollie a thumbs-up. The counselor with the bullhorn called for table seven to get lunch.

"That's us," Tess said. "This way." The twins followed her over to the buffet line. They each grabbed a tray and piled plates high with food.

Toby spotted them as they made their way back to the table. "Hey, Molly!" he called.

"Hi," Molly said.

"Let me see you get down!" Toby cried.

"Sorry, I can't dance right now," Molly said, nodding toward her tray.

"No prob," Toby said. Before Molly knew what was happening, he'd jumped up from his seat and grabbed her tray. "Now you can."

Molly felt her face flush. Her heart was beating as fast as a jackhammer. "Sorry, I don't know any dances," she said.

"Sure you do," Finn said. "You know how to square dance."

Molly thought back to the square dance she and Finn had learned in Colorado. She'd bowed to her partner, then crossed her arms and circled around.

It had been so much fun. She would've danced for hours, if PET hadn't honked its horn to pick her and Finn up.

But now Molly couldn't get her arms to cross or her feet to move. She felt everyone staring at her. What if she looked bad? What if everyone laughed at her? She was too scared to try.

"I'm sorry," Molly whispered. "I can't."

"No prob," Toby said again. "Here, you probably want this."

Molly nodded and took back her tray.

"Are you okay?" Tess asked.

"Yeah."

"Ready to head to the table?" Finn asked.

"Actually, I think I'm going to eat outside, if that's allowed," Molly said.

"Sure," Tess said. "Do you want us to go with you?"

"That's okay," Molly said. "I just need some quiet time."

"You definitely won't get any quiet in here," Finn said.

"I'll catch up with you guys after lunch," Molly said. She left the mess hall and headed outside to an empty picnic table. Her ears were still ringing from all the noise. But after a few minutes, she could hear the birds chirping and the leaves rustling the trees.

Ah, the glorious sounds of nature, Molly thought. She felt better already, and she took a bite of a chicken finger.

And then, there was another sound—an urgent whisper coming from behind an old shed.

"I've just gotten word that things are going from bad to worse," a man said.

Molly put down her chicken and strained to hear more.

"How much time do you think we have?" another voice asked. It sounded a lot like Danielle.

As quietly as she could, Molly got up from the picnic table and tiptoed closer to the shed. She peeked around the side.

Yep, it was Danielle. She was talking to a man whose back was to Molly. He was tall with black hair cut really close to his head. His shirt had "DIRECTOR" spelled out across the back.

"According to the fire marshal, it's still beyond the mountain," the director said. "We should be perfectly fine. But wind is unpredictable. If it shifts, we're going to need a backup plan."

"Should we tell the campers?" Danielle asked.

"Absolutely not," the director said. "We don't want anyone to worry if there's nothing to worry about. We'll tell them if and when the fire gets any closer."

Fire!

Molly's heart started to pound again. This had to be the work PET wanted her and Finn to do!

"Meanwhile, I'll send an email to the parents to let them know what's going on," the director continued.

"Of course, Jeremy," Danielle said. "I have a list of emergency contacts for every kid, and I'll spread the word to the other counselors."

"Excellent," Jeremy said. "And when you're . . ."

The sound of a distant helicopter drowned

out the rest of Jeremy's sentence. Molly took a tiny step closer.

A twig slapped her calf. "Ouch!" she said. Then she clapped a hand to her mouth.

Jeremy startled. "Did you hear that?" he asked.

"The helicopter?" Danielle asked.

"No. I thought I heard . . . ," Jeremy said. "Never mind. I will let you know as soon as I have any updates. For now, let's try to act normal in front of the campers."

"Okay," Danielle said.

Molly crept backward, watching the ground closely to make sure she didn't step on any more twigs. She picked up her tray and tiptoed toward the mess hall. As soon as she was far enough away, she began to run. She had to tell Finn what she'd heard. And fast!

Chapter 6

ANY WAY
THE WIND BLOWS

Molly went back to the mess hall, but it was impossible to talk to Finn alone. She had to wait until lunch was over, when everyone headed outside. The crowd gathered in a big field at the center of a large horseshoe of log cabins.

Molly pulled Finn off to the side. "I bet those are the cabins, don't you?" Finn asked.

"It doesn't matter," Molly said. "I have to tell you some—"

Before she could finish her sentence, she was interrupted by a counselor with a bull-horn. "All right, Eureka campers!" the counselor shouted. "You know what it's time for?"

"Capture the Flag!" the crowd shouted back.

"That's right," the counselor said. "If you are bunking in an even-numbered cabin, then you'll be on the gold team. If you're in an odd-numbered one, then you're on the blue team."

Finn turned to Molly. "Uh-oh. We don't have cabins."

"We've got bigger problems than that," Molly told him.

"What's wrong?" Finn asked.

"Oh hey, guys," Tess said. "There you are. I've been looking for you."

"Sorry, we weren't being good buddies," Finn said.

"Don't worry," Tess said. "The buddy system was just for the hike."

"Once a buddy, always a buddy," Finn said.

"Cool," Tess said. "Well, *buddies*, I have something for you. Just tell me what color you need." She held up four bandannas—two gold and two blue. "You wear these around your wrist so people know what team you're on."

"Thanks," Molly said, grabbing them.

"But you don't need—" Tess started.

"We'll be right back," Molly said. She stuffed the bandannas into her pocket and pulled Finn out of sight, behind a tree.

"You're being weird," Finn said. "What's going on?"

"I figured out our work," Molly said. "When I went outside to eat my lunch, I overheard Danielle and the camp director talking about a fire. It's over the mountain right now. But if the wind changes, it'll come *here,* and that's where we come in. We need to save the camp."

Finn shook his head. "PET knows we can't control the wind," he said. "We're no match for a fire."

"So what do *you* think we're supposed to do here?" Molly asked.

"C'mon, guys!" Tess called. "The game is about to start!"

"Right now I think we're supposed to play Capture the Flag with Tess and the others,"

Finn told his sister. He grabbed a bandanna from Molly's pocket. "I'll go on the blue team. You take gold."

He jogged over to the campers wearing blue bandannas, and Molly walked toward the gold team. Danielle had the bullhorn, and she shouted out the rules for anyone who didn't know them. "Teams, you have five minutes to hide your flags. The centerline is the stretch between cabins three and eight. As the name of the game suggests, whoever captures the other team's flag first wins. If you get tagged when you're in enemy territory, you'll end up in jail. One of your teammates will have to tag you to set you free. Got it?"

"Got it!" the campers all shouted.

"Now, friends, it's my pleasure to make the announcement you've all been waiting for," Danielle continued. "The team captains! For the gold team, it's Tamika!"

A girl in braids shrieked and pumped a fist in the air. Her teammates cheered.

"BOOOOOOO!" the blue team cried.

"And for the blue team, it's going to be . . . Finn!"

"Me?" Finn asked. "I get to be captain?"

"You sure do," Danielle said.

"Hooray, Finn!" Tess shouted.

"BOOOOOOO!" the gold team cried.

A siren blasted, marking the start of the game. Campers darted off in different directions, but Molly stayed put. She couldn't get her mind off the fire.

"Hey, new girl!" Tamika said, trotting up to Molly. "You're our guard. You think you can handle that?"

"Yeah. Okay," Molly said.

"Good. Go wait over by the jail in case someone gets tagged."

"Where's that?"

Tamika sighed and pointed toward a circle of logs. "Once someone lands in jail, don't let them get out. I'm undefeated in this game, and I don't plan to change that today. Capisce?"

Molly gulped and nodded. She jogged to the log circle. Finn was running around in blue territory. Molly shouted for him and waved her arms to try to get his attention. He was too caught up in the game to notice. She tried to send a message through twin-telepathy: *Get tagged and come over here to jail so we can make a plan.* But that didn't work, either.

Serafina was sent to jail. Molly guarded

her while she thought about things. She wasn't an expert in wildfires, but she'd read a book about them in first grade. She tried to remember what it'd said. . . .

Wildfires could start naturally, like from a lightning strike. But they were usually started by people who made a campfire and didn't put it out all the way. A small campfire could end up burning acres and acres of trees. Wildfires were worse when there was a dry spell, because it was easier for the fire to grow.

Molly remembered the patch of dead grass that Danielle had showed them. Dead grass was dry grass. There hadn't been enough rainfall and that was not good. Not good at all.

The breeze blew a strand of Molly's reddish-brown hair into her eyes.

Molly tucked her hair behind her ear. She

could hear a helicopter overhead. It sounded closer than before.

The fire was coming. Molly was sure of it. So how could she save the camp? Maybe build a barrier? But if she built something, the fire could burn it down. She could make it out of stones, which wouldn't burn as easily. But there was no way she'd be able to carry them—even if she did have Finn's help. And

right then Finn was too busy trying to capture the flag.

"Hey, Molly!" Tamika shouted. "You let
the prisoner out!"

Molly spun around and looked behind
her. Serafina was gone. Across the field, she
gave Finn and Tess high fives.

"I'm really sorry," Molly told Tamika. "I
got distracted."

"Do I need to replace you as guard?" Tamika asked. "This is important work, you know."

Tamika had said the magic word: "work." But Molly was almost certain that guarding the gold team's jail was *not* the work PET had in mind.

WHOOP! WHOOP! WHOOP! a siren sounded.

"Attention, Eureka campers and staff members!" Jeremy shouted into the bullhorn. "This game of Capture the Flag has officially come to an end!"

"But no one won yet!" Tamika cried.

"I'm calling an emergency camp meeting at the flagpole," Jeremy said. "Right now!"

Chapter 7

EMERGENCY CAMP MEETING

A pit of dread settled in Molly's stomach. She was pretty sure she knew what this emergency meeting was about.

"I'm sorry we had to cut the game short, campers," Jeremy said. "But we've learned there's a fire in the area."

There was a collective gasp. Everyone started talking at once.

"Quiet down, please!" Jeremy said. "It's

going to be okay. As a precaution, the fire marshal wants us to leave the campground right away. I know we usually travel to and from camp on buses. But we can't risk the trip through the mountains. Our safest route today will be across the water."

"You mean we have to *swim* out of here?" Tess asked.

"I'm a pretty strong swimmer," Tamika said. "I'm in the kingfish group, after all. But it's still way too far—even for me."

"No one is expected to swim," Jeremy said. "We have enough canoes and rowboats for everyone, as well as life jackets, which everyone is required to wear—no exceptions. As you've probably noticed, the wind has picked up, which makes the water a bit rough."

Nervous murmurs passed through the crowd.

"Too bad the camp bus doesn't travel on the *information superhighway* like PET does," Finn whispered to Molly. "We'd be out of here in a flash."

"We need to do this in an organized way," Jeremy said. "We're going to head to the lake and—"

"Wait," Toby said. "Shouldn't we go to the bunks first to get our stuff, and then go to the dock?"

"Your stuff is staying here," Jeremy said.

"But what about my lucky track sneakers?" Toby asked.

"And my charm bracelet?" Tamika said.

"And the tie-dye shirt I made yesterday?" another camper asked.

Danielle took the bullhorn from Jeremy. "Hey, friends," she said. "I know your stuff is important to you. But it's too heavy to bring on canoes and rowboats, and it'd take up too much space. Besides, packing takes time that we don't have."

"How close is the fire?" Serafina asked in a shaky voice.

Danielle handed the bullhorn back to Jeremy. "It's close enough that Camp Eureka has been declared a mandatory evacuation zone," he said. "Once it's declared a safe zone again, we'll all come back here. For now, anyone in the guppy swim group, gather by the yellow cone. Dolphins, you're by the green cone. And kingfish, go to the orange cone."

The crowd started to move. "We're not in a swim group," Finn whispered to Molly.

"We joined up with Capture the Flag teams, even though we didn't have cabins," she said.

"That's true," Finn agreed.

"But I still think staying here and fighting the fire might be our work," Molly added.

"We don't have any firefighter training," Finn said. "We don't even have the right clothes."

Molly looked down at her camp uniform. Finn was right. Shorts and a T-shirt were not good firefighting clothes.

"Besides," Finn went on. "If it's not really our work, we'll be stuck here in a fire, and that's too dangerous. We have to go. Think of the birds."

"What birds?" Molly asked.

"The ones we saw this morning," Finn

said. "Something on the ground was making them scared, so they flew up to get away."

"Oh, the quail," Molly said. She took a deep breath and detected a whiff of smoke in the air. "Okay, let's go," she said.

She and Finn followed the crowd down to the lake. When they reached the boathouse, they hid behind a tree while the counselors did a head count of the swim groups. Since the twins didn't actually belong to any swim group, they didn't want to mess up the count.

"Listen up, Eureka campers," Jeremy said. "We're going to assign four people to each rowboat and two per canoe. If you're in the guppy or dolphin swim groups, you must go with an adult—either a counselor or a staff member. Everyone, grab a life jacket."

The crowd surged toward the boathouse door. "You're crushing me!" someone shouted.

"FREEZE!" Jeremy shouted. "We need to respect each other and be orderly."

Finn stepped out from behind the tree. "Hey, Jeremy, my sister, Molly, and I can hand out the life jackets," he said.

"Thank you . . . thank you . . ."

"Finn," Finn supplied.

"Everyone, line up in front of Molly and Finn," Jeremy said.

The twins got to work handing out life jackets and making sure everyone was safely clipped in. They put their own life jackets on last, clipping the buckles and adjusting the straps around their waists so they fit snugly.

"All right," Danielle said. "Swim groups to your cones."

"So what cone should we go to?" Finn asked.

"Whichever one Tess is in," Molly said. "Do you see her?"

"Um ...," Finn said. "No, I don't."

"Me neither," Molly said. "When did you see her last?"

"Hmm, let me think," Finn said. "She high-fived Serafina after she broke out of jail."

"You haven't seen her since Capture the Flag?" Molly asked.

"Yeah," Finn said. "Wait, no. That's not right. She was at the emergency meeting. She asked a question about having to swim."

"Oh, right," Molly said. "So we know she was at the flagpole. We'll start looking there."

"The fire is coming," Finn said. "The boats are leaving."

"But we're Tess's buddies," Molly reminded him. "Once a buddy, always a buddy. Right?"

"That's right," Finn said. "Let's go."

Chapter 8

BIRD'S-EYE VIEW

Another helicopter flew by, and ripples spread across the water.

"I feel terrible that we lost Tess," Molly said.

"We're gonna fix that right now," Finn said.

There was no time to waste. The twins tiptoed around the boathouse. Once they were out of sight of the counselors and other campers, they broke into a run.

But when they got to the flagpole, there was no sign of Tess.

Molly and Finn shouted for her anyway. "TESS! TESS! TESSSSSSSSS!"

Tess didn't answer. The only sounds were the flag flapping wildly in the breeze and the roar of the helicopter propellers spinning overhead.

"Maybe there was something Tess didn't want to leave behind, even though Jeremy said we couldn't take anything with us," Finn said. "Let's go check her cabin."

They raced back to the horseshoe of log cabins.

"Do you know which one is Tess's?" Molly asked.

"No," Finn said. "How about you check

the ones on the left, and I'll take the ones on the right?"

"You got it," Molly said.

She ducked into Cabin 1. On the opposite side of the field, Finn headed into Cabin 10. "TESS!" they both shouted.

There wasn't any answer.

They each made their way down the line: Cabins 2 and 9. Cabins 3 and 8. Cabins 4 and 7. Finally cabins 5 and 6.

But Tess wasn't in any of them.

Molly could feel her heart beating underneath her life jacket. "The fire is getting closer," she said. "I can smell it."

"Me too," Finn said. "But Tess has to be around here somewhere. She couldn't have just disappeared. She's not a magic camper, like PET. She's an ordinary kid, like us."

"Where should we go next?" Molly asked.

"The mess hall," Finn said. "She could've run in there to get snacks for the trip."

Molly doubted that Tess would worry about food during a fire emergency, but she didn't have a better idea. She and Finn raced to the mess hall. Inside, it was eerily quiet. The chairs were stacked up on the tables. The room smelled like lemon cleaner.

"TESS!" they called out.

The sound of their voices echoed through the empty room.

"She's not here," Molly said. "What if she really *did* have a bad appendix? She could be stuck somewhere feeling very sick!"

"You said her stomachache was in the wrong place for it to be her appendix," Finn said. "Besides, she felt better after swimming time was over. She went on the hike and everything."

"Maybe I was wrong about the wrong place," Molly said. "I'm not a doctor. I'm really worried about her, and we're running out of time."

"I'm worried, too," Finn said. "But look here."

He tapped the map of Camp Eureka that was posted by the mess hall door.

"We're going to check every single place that's left till we find Tess," Finn said. "It'll go faster if we split up. You take the theater. I'll take the canteen. We'll meet back at the flag-pole in five minutes, no matter what."

"No matter what," Molly agreed.

Finn put his hand on the door handle. "You know, it's too bad we're not like those quail that can fly when they sense danger. Then we'd be able to stick together and see the whole camp."

And with that, he yanked the door open.

"Wait," Molly said. "That's exactly what we need to do! We're going to be like the quail and get a bird's-eye view of the whole camp!"

"I hate to point this out," Finn said, "but we don't have wings."

"We don't need them," Molly said. "Remember what Tess told us about the treehouse? She said she could see the whole camp from up there. It's right by the . . . by the . . ."

"By the what?" Finn asked.

"I can't remember," Molly said.

"I'll check the map," Finn said. He ran his finger along all the different places. "The volleyball court, the dance studio, the ropes course . . . I don't see it."

"The ropes course!" Molly said. "That's it! Tess said the treehouse was right by the ropes course."

WHOOP WHOOP WHOOP! the alarm sounded.

Jeremy's voice boomed through the speakers. "All remaining staff members to the dock! The boats are leaving in five minutes! I repeat: the boats are leaving in five minutes!"

"Five minutes," Finn moaned. "That's practically no time at all."

Molly grabbed Finn's hand. "C'mon! Let's hope we're not too late!"

Chapter 9

THE TREEHOUSE

The twins ran faster than they'd ever run before. They were at the base of the treehouse in under a minute. But when they got there . . .

"How do we get up?" Finn asked.

"There's got to be a rope or a ladder or something," Molly said.

"I don't see anything. Maybe this isn't the right tree."

"Of course it is. Look up—see the floor of the treehouse? That hole must be the door."

"So . . . we're just supposed to climb up?"

"I guess."

"I'll go first," Finn said.

The wind whipped around them. The helicopters roared overhead. Finn tried not to let all that distract him. It was like when his Little League team played the championship game during the Fourth of July fireworks.

He could hear Coach Russo's voice in his head saying, "Focus." Finn gripped the trunk of the tree. He lifted up a foot.

"Hey!" a voice called. "You guys better go to the lake!"

"Tess!" Molly said. "Is that you?"

Tess peered out through the hole in the floor of the treehouse.

"Holy guacamole, it *is* you!" Finn said. "We've been looking all over for you. Have you been here all along?"

"I—" Tess started.

"Tell us later," Molly said. "We need to get to the dock. Now."

"That's right," Finn said. "The boats are leaving in a few minutes."

"You need to go without me," Tess said.

"No way!" Molly cried. "We're not leaving without you!"

Tess didn't reply.

"I'm going to try climbing the tree again," Finn said.

But before he put his hands back on the tree, a rope ladder dropped down through the treehouse floor. Finn scrambled up, and Molly was right behind him.

Tess was sitting on the treehouse floor. Her eyes were red and puffy. "I'm sorry about this," she said. "But I can't go on a boat."

"Why?" Molly asked. "Does your stomach hurt again?"

Tess shook her head. "No. It's worse than that. Way worse. I can't . . . I can't swim." She buried her face in her hands.

"Don't worry, Tess," Finn said. "That's what life jackets are for."

Tess took her hands off her face, but she shook her head again. "I'm too scared of the water," she said. "I can't even dog-paddle. I didn't take the swim test, because I didn't want everyone to see. I never even got put in a swim group. I knew when they counted the guppies, dolphins, and kingfish, they wouldn't know I was missing. If I stay up here, the fire might not be able to reach me. I'll be safe from the fire and safe from drowning."

"Oh, Tess," Molly said. "I understand how you feel about going in the water."

"You don't know how to swim, either?" Tess asked.

"No, I do," Molly said.

"So you can't really understand how I'm feeling," Tess said.

"Maybe not about swimming," Molly said. "But I know what it feels like to be scared to do something that everyone else wants me to do. It happens to me a lot. It even happened today."

"When?" Finn asked.

"Remember back at the mess hall when

everyone was trying to get me to dance?"

"Oh yeah," Finn said, and Tess nodded.

"I like dancing," Molly said. "But at that moment, it felt like my feet were glued to the floor. My face got hot. My heart was beating as fast as those helicopter propellers out there. What if I'm actually a bad dancer? I didn't want anyone to see."

"That's how I feel right now," Tess said. "I guess you *do* know."

"I also know that you can get on that boat anyway," Molly said.

"But you didn't even get up and dance!" Tess said.

"I hate to agree with her on this, but she's right," Finn said.

"I should have," Molly said. "I should have faced my fears, and you should, too."

"I'll think about it," Tess said.

"Think fast," Finn said. "This treehouse isn't going to keep us safe from the fire. Trees are made of wood, after all."

"Finn and I will be with you in the boat the whole time," Molly said. "What do you say?"

"I—" Tess started, and Molly and Finn held their breath. "I'll try," she said.

"Great!" Finn cried. "Let's go right now." He scooted toward the hole in the floor. "This really is a great view of the whole camp. I can see Danielle."

"Hey, Danielle!" Molly shouted.

But between the distance and the helicopters in the background, Danielle couldn't hear.

All together, they shouted, "HEY, DANIELLE!"

Danielle turned around.

"Wait for us! We're coming!" they called,
and then they scrambled down the ladder.

Chapter 10

GREAT ESCAPE

Molly, Finn, and Tess sprinted across the grass.

Danielle's usually sun-kissed face had gone nearly as white as a sheet. "What were you doing up in the treehouse?" she asked.

"I'm sorry," Tess said. "It was my—"

"It was *my* fault," Molly broke in. "I heard the view was great up there, and I wanted to see it. Finn and Tess figured out that's where I'd gone, and they came to rescue me."

"That was really dangerous of all *three* of you," Danielle said. "What if we had left without you?"

A gust of wind blew. The smell of smoke grew stronger. Finn coughed.

"Pull your T-shirts over your mouths," Danielle said.

"How about these?" Molly asked. She pulled the last two blue and gold bandannas out of her pocket and handed them to Danielle and Tess. Everyone tied them over their noses and mouths.

"It's so dark," Finn said. "I didn't realize how late it had gotten."

"It's not late," Danielle said. "The smoke

clouds are blocking the sun. We need to get out of here."

Tess put on a life jacket. She and the twins climbed into the very last rowboat. Then Danielle gave the boat a shove. She jogged through the water and climbed in with them. There were two oars at the bottom of the boat, and Danielle grabbed one.

"I'll take the other," Finn offered.

"You can switch off with the girls if you get tired," Danielle said.

"Don't worry, you won't have to do any rowing," Molly told Tess. "Finn and I can take turns."

"I'll be fine getting us all the way across," Finn said. "I have a really strong pitching arm."

Molly and Tess huddled together. "It's

going to be okay," Molly said. "All you have to do is sit here."

"Plus not fall in," Tess replied.

"You can do it."

Finn lifted his oar out of the water and dipped it in again. The water was choppy, and it was getting harder and harder to keep up with Danielle's pace. Finn clutched the end of the oar with both hands and lifted it in and out, in and out.

"Help," Finn said. "Something is caught on my oar!"

Danielle glanced over as Finn heaved it out of the water. "Looks okay to me," she told him.

"But it's gotten so heavy," he said.

"You've been working hard," Danielle said. "It's okay to give one of the girls a turn."

"I'll go," Molly said. She got up on her knees to scoot over and switch seats. "Whoa," she said.

"What's wrong?" Tess asked.

"I feel dizzy," Molly said.

"Hmm," Danielle said. "Your face looks a bit green."

"You're seasick, aren't you?" Finn asked.

"I think so," Molly said.

"I'd tell you to breathe in the fresh air, but there isn't much of that to go around. Try closing your eyes," Danielle said.

"But I can't close my eyes and paddle for Finn at the same time," Molly said.

"It's okay," Finn said. He heaved the oar out again, panting. "I'll keep going."

Tess took a deep breath. "I'll do it," she said.

"No . . . I can . . . ," Molly said. But she swayed in her seat.

"It's okay, Molly," Tess said. "I can do this."

Finn pulled his oar back into the boat and handed it to Tess. She settled into the seat across from Danielle.

Finn moved to sit beside his sister. "You're not going to puke on me, are you?" he asked.

"I'll try not to," Molly said. She kept her

eyes closed. The air still smelled of smoke, and the waves hadn't quieted down. But at least the breeze on her cheeks made her feel a little better.

A few minutes passed. "Molly," Finn whispered. "Look."

Molly's eyes popped open, and she looked across the boat where Finn was pointing. Tess was dipping her oar in and out, in and out. She didn't look scared. She looked determined.

And just a few yards behind her was the best sight of all—the shore.

Chapter 11

BRAVE

Jeremy waded into the water and helped pull the rowboat to shore. Danielle and the kids climbed out and joined the rest of the Camp Eureka campers and counselors.

"How are you feeling, Molly?" Tess asked.

"Better now that we're on dry land," Molly said. "How are *you* feeling?"

"I feel good." Tess smiled.

"You did great," Finn said. "You're really strong—and brave."

"You're *all* strong and brave," Danielle said.

"What took you so long?" Jeremy asked.

The twins and Tess looked at each other nervously.

"We accidentally took the scenic route," Danielle said. She winked at the twins and Tess.

"It still smells like smoke," Finn said. "I thought we came here to escape the fire."

"Crossing the lake was step one," Jeremy said. "Now we need to get on the buses."

"But you said the roads weren't safe," Tess said.

"The roads out of camp weren't safe, but there's a clear path to San Francisco from here," Jeremy explained. "I arranged for your parents to meet us there."

"*Our* parents?" Molly asked.

She and Finn shared a worried look. Had Jeremy told their parents they were in California? What would they think? Would they even believe him?

"I sent an email to every parent of a camper on the Camp Eureka roster to let them know about our change of plans," Jeremy said.

The twins breathed a sigh of relief. They weren't on the camp roster. That meant their parents still didn't know where they were.

But what about PET?

"Maybe we shouldn't get on the bus," Finn whispered to his sister. "After all, we already found Tess and helped her across the lake. Wasn't that our work?"

"Definitely," Molly said. "But the helicopters are so loud over here, we probably won't hear PET's beep."

"Let's go, friends," Danielle called. "We've got to hit the road!"

She jumped up the bus steps, and the campers started to climb on behind her.

"If PET can't find us, then we'll be stuck in California," Molly said. "How will we explain that to Mom and Dad?"

"C'mon, you two," Danielle called to the twins. "I'm not leaving you behind again."

"We have to go. We have no choice," Finn told Molly.

He and Molly climbed aboard. Danielle had saved two seats for them up front. Molly closed her eyes again and let the breeze from the air conditioner dance on her face. The campers sang the Camp Eureka song:

"Camp Eureka is the best place to make new friends. Wherever we go, whatever we do, we'll be together till the end!"

Without even trying, Molly realized she'd memorized all the words.

A little while later, Finn shook her shoulder. "Wake up!"

"I'm not sleeping," Molly said, opening her eyes.

"Look out the window!"

Bridge columns were zipping by—orange-gold-colored bridge columns—peeking through thick clouds.

"Oh my goodness!" Molly cried. "Are we on the Golden Gate Bridge?"

"We sure are," Tess said from the row behind them.

The bus crossed the bridge and wound through the city streets. "Holy guacamole, this is the steepest street I've ever been on," Finn said. "I hope the bus can make it to the top."

They got to the crest of the hill.

"Uh-oh," Molly said. "Now we have to go down. The brakes better work!"

"You guys haven't been to San Francisco before, have you?" Tess asked.

Finn and Molly shook their heads. The bus turned into a parking lot and rumbled to a stop.

"Everyone out," Jeremy said, and the campers bounded outside.

"Smell that?" Danielle asked.

"What?" Finn asked.

"Fresh, smoke-free air!"

"I'm surprised we can't smell the fire anymore," Molly said. "The bridge was so smoky."

Danielle laughed. "That wasn't smoke," she said. "That was the famous San Francisco fog. Don't worry—we're a safe ways away from the fire."

99

"Your parents are meeting us here in Golden Gate Park," Jeremy told the crowd. "But since we're early, I've arranged a surprise for you. Come this way."

"Friends, please stick with your buddies," Danielle added.

Molly and Finn stuck with Tess and followed the crowd to a carousel. There weren't just horses to ride, but also frogs, dogs, roosters, and pigs!

"I claim the dragon!" Toby said.

"I claim the ostrich," Serafina said.

"I think we should ride horses, for old times' sake," Molly told Finn. "That one looks like Dasha, don't you think?"

"Who's Dasha?" Tess asked.

"Oh, just a horse I once rode," Molly said.

"It *does* look like Dasha," Finn said. "But

don't you have something else you need to do first?"

"Huh?"

"Oh, right," Tess said. "You definitely have something you need to do—you need to get DOWN!"

Tess was so loud that the other kids all turned to watch.

Molly felt her cheeks burning and her heart racing. She knew it was partly because she felt afraid. But there was another part: she felt brave.

Brave from when she'd ridden Dasha in Colorado.

Brave from when she'd flown in a helicopter in New York.

Brave from when she'd shinnied up a rope ladder in Texas.

And brave from watching Tess paddle the rowboat safely out of Camp Eureka.

Molly had been afraid all those times. But she'd faced her fears, and it had been worth it. Now she was ready to face them again, and she shuffled her feet like in a square dance.

"D-O-W-N," all the campers cheered. "That's the way we get down!"

Molly linked elbows with Tess. They spun in a circle. Molly laughed so hard that tears pricked the corners of her eyes.

"That was great," Finn said.

"It sure was," Tess agreed. "Let's ride the carousel!"

But right then, a honk sounded off in the distance.

"Wait, Tess," Molly said. "I have something to give to you."

Molly untied the blue-and-gold bracelet from her wrist and handed it to her new friend.

"Thanks!" Tess said. "I love it."

PET honked again.

"C'mon!" Tess said. She skipped over to the ride and picked a fierce-looking lion to sit on. The music started to play, and the carousel began to turn.

Once Tess's lion had spun out of sight, the twins took off toward the parking lot to catch their ride home.

Chapter 12

HOMEWARD BOUND

The camper was parked on the far side of the parking lot, under a tall, lean redwood tree. When Molly and Finn got closer, the door swung open and they climbed in. They clicked their seat belts into place. PET's screen lit up like a fireworks show. The camper rocked from side to side. Finn pressed his face to the window as they rose into the air.

"The bridge looks so small from up here,"

he said. "Like the size of a Lego."

As they flew on, dark gray clouds made it impossible to see anything. "Wow, the famous San Francisco fog is even thicker than before," Molly said.

"Unfortunately, that's smoke from the wildfires," PET said.

"The fire is so much bigger than I thought it'd be," Finn said.

"I know," Molly said. "All day long, we were trying to figure out the work we had to do. But now I'm thinking about the work the firefighters are doing down there."

"They cut back the brush and grass to try to stop the fire from spreading farther," PET said. "And they battle it from the sky, too—they drop water and chemicals from planes and helicopters."

"That's why we heard all those helicopters!" Finn said. "I thought they were just up there to see where the fire was."

"Hey, PET. Do you think the firefighters will be able to finish their work soon?" Molly asked.

"It takes a long time to contain a wildfire," PET said.

"More than a day?" Finn asked.

"Sometimes weeks."

"Weeks?"

"Or even months."

"Months?"

"I wish there was more we could do to help," Molly said.

"You can do your best to prevent them in the future," PET said. "Never play with matches or lighters."

"We won't," Finn said. "We promise."

"And if you go camping, only start fires in designated campfire areas. Watch the fire carefully, and make sure to extinguish the flames completely before you leave."

A few minutes later, the camper landed with a thud. Molly peeked out her window and saw their familiar white house and hunter-green mailbox.

"Thanks for the ride home, PET," she said.

"My pleasure," PET said. "You did your work well today, kids."

"Thanks, PET," Finn said.

"You'll be back tomorrow, right?" Molly asked.

"I am not allowed to say," PET said.

"Not allowed?" Molly asked. "Who made that rule? Professor Vega?"

But Molly never got an answer. PET's screen shut off. Everything was quiet.

Molly and Finn unbuckled their seat belts and walked through the camper, past the couch and the table and the television. They stopped in front of the map of the world. Molly picked up a red pushpin and stuck it in California.

"Look at all the places we've been,"

Finn said. "Colorado, New York, Texas, and now California. Can you believe it's only Tuesday?"

"Let's go get some breakfast," Molly said. "I have a feeling it's going to be a busy week."

AUTHORS' NOTE

Thank you for joining the Parker twins for their fourth adventure! The Magic on the Map books are made-up stories, but Molly and Finn faced a very real-life threat in *Escape from Camp California*—wildfires.

Wildfires have become more common and more destructive than ever before. A big reason for this is something you may have heard of—something called climate change.

It's important to know that climate is different from weather. Weather changes from day to day. Climate is the weather patterns over a long period of time. And climate change is the process of our planet heating up overall. Certain human-made gases, like carbon dioxide, trap heat inside the earth's atmosphere. That makes the earth get warmer. Since 1880, the overall temperature of the earth has risen by over 1°F.

One degree doesn't sound like a lot, but it

makes a big difference. Scientists have observed icebergs melting and sea levels rising. As Molly and Finn learned, the earth is also experiencing longer dry spells. When the ground is dry, it's easier for fires to spread.

The good news is, there are things you can do to fight climate change. You can reduce the amount of energy you use—turn the lights out when you leave a room, use fewer electronics (read books instead!), and walk or ride your bike to your friend's house if it's not too far away. This will reduce the amount of carbon dioxide that's released into the atmosphere. You can also re-member PET's wildfire tips: Never play with matches or lighters. If you go camping, only start fires in designated campfire areas, and make sure to extinguish the flames completely before you leave.

If you want to learn more about climate change, we recommend checking out Kids

Against Climate Change. Learn more about this at kidsagainstclimatechange.co.

We hope you enjoy your travels—both real and made-up!

Your friends,
Courtney & Bianca

California State Facts

- The California state tree is the redwood. The state flower is the golden poppy, and the state bird is the California quail.

- The California state flag looks like this:

- The official colors of California are blue and gold.

- Sacramento is the state capital.

- Sequoia National Park, in the southern Sierra Nevada Mountain range, is home to one of the largest living trees—a Sequoia redwood tree. Its name is General Sherman, and its circumference is over 100 feet! That's more than the height of ten elephants combined!

- The Golden Gate Bridge connects the city of

San Francisco to Marin County and is one of the seven wonders of the modern world. It's actually more orange than gold, but it looks golden when the sun hits it.

✪ California is called the Golden State because gold was discovered at Sutter's Mill sawmill in 1849, which caused the famous California gold rush of 1849. The miners were called the 49ers, which is also the name of San Francisco's football team.

✪ The state motto is "Eureka!" which means "I have found it!"

✪ California is also known for its iconic film industry and studios. People come from all over the world to "make it" in Hollywood.

PET's favorite California fact:

✪ Fog is common in the San Francisco Bay Area because the hot Northern California air meets the cold ocean air, creating a fog effect, which often leads to travel alerts. But PET can fly through the fog, no problem!

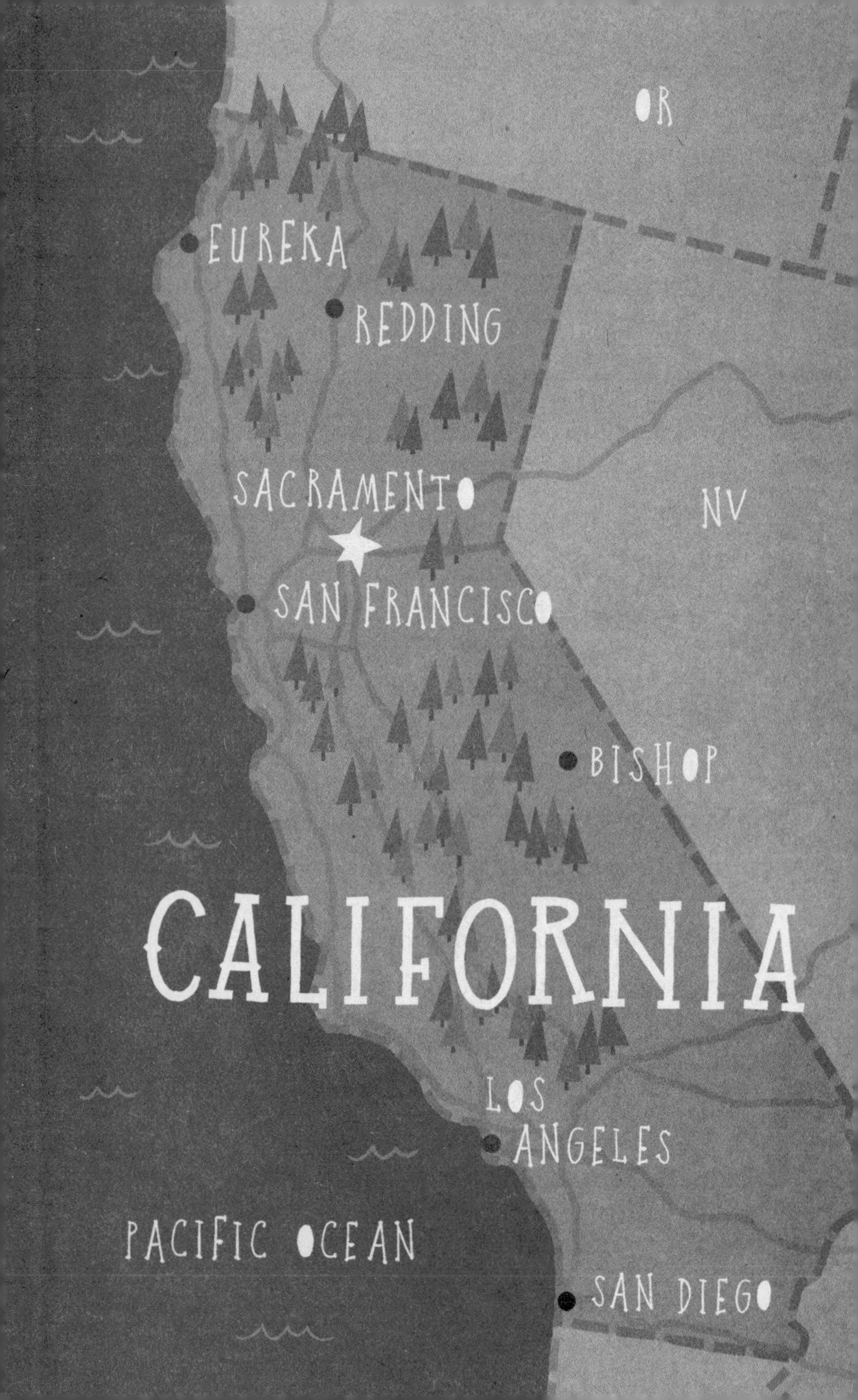
OR
EUREKA
REDDING
SACRAMENTO
NV
SAN FRANCISCO
BISHOP
CALIFORNIA
LOS ANGELES
PACIFIC OCEAN
SAN DIEGO

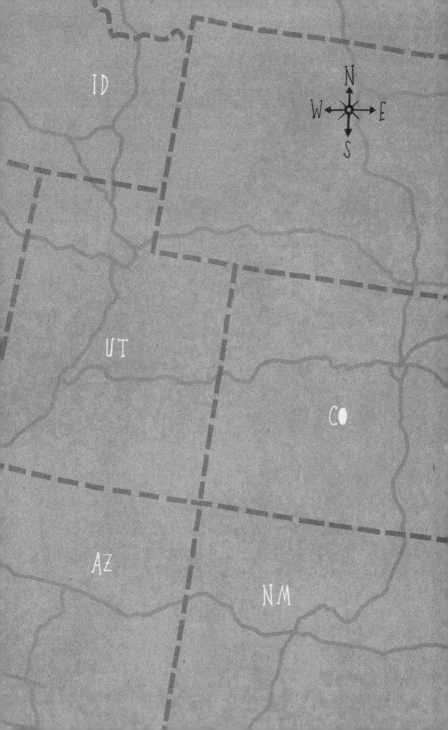

Travel with Finn and Molly in the

MAGIC ON THE MAP books!

Have you read them all?

Where will Finn and Molly go next?

★